Whisker's Great Adventure

For
Christopher, Charlie and Andrew

'This son of mine
was dead and is alive again;
he was lost and is found.'
THE PARABLE OF
THE PRODIGAL SON

Whisker's
Great Adventure

MERYL DONEY

Illustrated by William Geldart

Wm. B. Eerdmans Publishing Co.
Grand Rapids, Michigan

Text © 1994 Meryl Doney
Illustrations © 1994 William Geldart

Published by arrangement with Hodder Religious Books

The author and illustrator asserts the moral right to be
identified as the author and illustrator of this work

First Published 1994 in the U.K. by Hodder and Stoughton

This edition published 1996 by
William B. Eerdmans Publishing Co.
255 Jefferson Ave. S.E., Grand Rapids, Michigan 49503

00 99 98 97 96   7 6 5 4 3 2

Library of Congress Cataloging-in-Publication Data

Doney, Meryl, 1942-
Whisker's great adventure / Meryl Doney ;
illustrated by William Geldart.
p.   cm.
Summary: In this retelling of the parable of the prodigal son,
Whiskers, a baby otter, disobeys his father and gets into
serious trouble before being rescued.
ISBN 0-8028-5124-X (cloth : alk. paper)
ISBN 0-8028-5064-2 (pbk. : alk. paper)
[1. Otters — Fiction. 2. Obedience — Fiction. 3. Parables.]
I. Geldart, Bill, ill. II. Title
PZ7.D7165Wh 1996
[E] — dc20   95-41918
                                                  CIP
                                                  AC

Whisker the Otter was born in a nest
on the riverbank. He and his brother and two
sisters loved to play. Soon the nest was full of
flying feet and fur.

One day, Father and Mother took
them down to the river's edge.
'Oooh, it looks cold,'
squeaked the other cubs.
'It looks exciting,' said Whisker.

Father Otter took each cub
gently in his mouth and
dunked it in the water.
Soon they were all
tumbling and splashing,
rolling over and over
and pretending to
bite each other.

'Look at me,' squeaked Whisker.
'I'm swimming!'
He gulped as the current caught
him and carried him downstream.

Suddenly Whisker's head caught fast in
the branches of a tree. His feet flew up in
the air. 'Aaargh!' he spluttered.
'What happened?'

All the family laughed and laughed.

When Father Otter had rescued Whisker, he said to his children, 'This is the first lesson you must learn. The river is your friend, but there are many dangers:

Beware the downstream danger-lands,
The hounds that rip and tear.
Beware the weasel's needle teeth,
The wildcat's deadly stare.
Always travel upstream – and beware!'

'Always travel upstream,' three small otters chorused, 'and beware.'

'Ha!' Whisker said loudly. 'I'm not afraid of dangers.'

One morning there
came a distant howl.
Father raised his snout
and sniffed the air.

'The hounds are
running,' he said.

A shiver ran
through the cubs as
they snuggled deeper
into the nest.

Whisker was not impressed.
'I want to see the world,' he thought.
'I don't want to stay here.'

He crept to the door of the nest
and looked out. Warm sunlight
slanted through the trees and
sparkled on the surface
of the river.

Whisker peered upstream. White water
tumbled over dark rocks. But downstream,
the water flowed smoothly between soft
green banks. Whisker slid into
the water and began to swim
– downstream.

Before long he stopped to listen. From far away he could hear excited barking and the drumming of many paws along the riverbank.

Suddenly the hounds were all around him, splashing in the river and nosing into every hole in the bank. Whisker froze. His fur stood out all over his body. He leaped from the water and began to run.

Finally he stopped,
gasping for breath.
He sniffed the air.
There was no scent,
no sound.
Whisker was alone.

'What have we here?'
A large weasel bounded down the bank.
  'A baby otter, I do believe!' said another.
Several more weasels appeared
and crowded round Whisker.
He could see their
needle-sharp teeth.
  'What shall we do
with this one?'
  'Bit too fat for
us weasels, but a
nice mouthful
for the Striped One.'

Whisker didn't wait
to meet the Striped
One. He leaped into
the water and swam
for his life.

All that day Whisker swam and walked, walked and swam. At last, exhausted, he pulled himself out of the water. The sun had set, and he could see yellow eyes in the dark forest.

Whisker lay against
a great tree trunk.
  'I wish I was home,'
he said to himself.
And he began to cry.

'What's wrong?'
said a gentle voice.
A white deer stood
among the trees.
'I...I'm lost,' Whisker
sniffed. 'I ran away.
I went downstream.
And now the Striped
One's after me.'

'The way home is upstream,'
the deer said. 'Be brave.
Go back the way you came.
You haven't been forgotten.'

Whisker looked upstream.
Of course that was the way
home. He set off bravely.

Suddenly he froze.
Crouched on a rock above him
was a great, striped wildcat.
It had swept-back ears, yellow
teeth, and huge, staring eyes.
The Striped One!
It glared at Whisker and
swayed from side to side,
ready to pounce.

At that moment something long and dark sprang
from the river. In a shower of spray it hurled itself
towards the wildcat. There was a furious fight.
Whisker watched, shaking with fear.

Then suddenly it was all over.
The wildcat turned and bounded away.

'Father!'
Whisker cried. 'Are you hurt?'
'I'll be all right,' Father said.
'I'm so glad I've found you,' and he licked Whisker all over.
'How did you find me?' Whisker asked.
'I have been searching for you ever since you left home,' Father replied.

When they
had recovered,
Whisker and Father Otter
began the long journey home.
Sometimes they ran along the bank.
Sometimes they swam upstream.

At last they were home.
'Whisker!' the cubs
shouted. 'Father! You've
come back! Where did
you find him?'
'Downstream,' said
Father. 'A long way
downstream.'
Whisker ran to Mother
Otter and buried his
head in her fur.

Safe in the nest, Whisker told his family
about his adventure:
about the hounds ready to rip and tear;
about the weasels,' needle teeth;
and the fight with the terrible
Striped One.
As the cubs listened, their eyes
grew round with fright.

'Then Father came
and found me,'
Whisker said with
a happy smile.